SIMON PUTTOCK was born in New Zealand and travelled all over the world as a child. He has had a varied career, from cinema projectionist to sound engineer to singer/ songwriter and cabaret club D.J. He has written over 30 books for children.

HOLLY SWAIN is a children's book illustrator, living in Hove with her husband Matt. As a child she always loved to draw, making up characters and their worlds. She used to have a huge roll of paper under her bed that she constantly drew on which gradually got smaller and smaller, by which time she was big enough to go to college. Holly studied Illustration at UWE Bristol and then did an MA in Brighton.

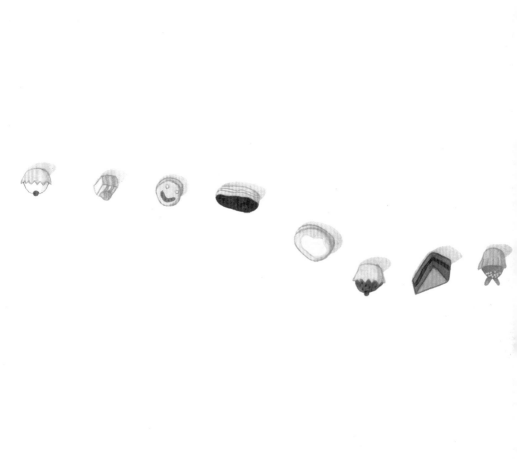

For Rosemary Canter, with love - S.P.
For Rose, with love - H.S.

Text copyright © Simon Puttock 2006, 2014
Illustrations copyright © Holly Swain 2006, 2014

The rights of Simon Puttock and Holly Swain to be identified respectively
as the author and illustrator of this Work have been asserted by them in
accordance with the Copyright, Designs and Patent Act, 1988.

First published in Great Britain and in the USA in 2006.
This early reader edition published in Great Britain in 2014 by
Frances Lincoln Children's Books,
74-77 White Lion Street, London, N1 9PF
www.franceslincoln.com

A CIP catalogue record for this book is available from the British Library.

ISBN 978-1-84780-545-4

Printed in China

1 3 5 7 9 8 6 4 2

MISS
FOX

Simon Puttock
Holly Swain

F
FRANCES LINCOLN
CHILDREN'S BOOKS

Welcome to Niceville

It was the first day of school. Miss Fox was a
teacher, but she had no children to teach. She
strolled into Niceville.

It looked like a comfy sort of, cosy sort of place. So, Miss Fox stopped and asked a shopkeeper the way to Niceville School.

Miss Fox smiled her sweetest smile at Mr Billy,
the head teacher.
She told him, "I am the most wonderful teacher in the
world. You need me to teach your dear little children."
Mr. Billy gave Miss Fox the job at once.

"I am Miss Felicity Fox, and I am a wonderful teacher."
"Ooh!" gasped everyone in Class Two. Everyone,
that is, but Lily Lamb. Lily Lamb was a clever girl.
She always asked annoying questions, and she
never ever did what she was told. "Bah!" said Lily.
"Silly Foxy! Who does she think she is?"
And she went on making aeroplanes.

But Miss Fox was a wonderful teacher. Every day she brought the children treats: doughnuts, cream buns and little cakes with pink icing.
"Miss Fox is the best," Class Two agreed.

"Bah!" said Lily Lamb. "You're all greedy-weedies. Miss Fox never eats treats herself. I wonder what she does like to eat . . . ?"

At playtimes, Miss Fox kept the children indoors and told them tales of kind, beautiful foxes doing wonderful things.

"Ooh!" said Class Two. "Terrific story!"

"Bah! Bah - soppy!" said Lily Lamb.

And she sneaked out to play hopscotch all by herself.
Everyone in Class Two was happy, well-fed and
lazy. But not Lily Lamb. She was just as cross and
annoying and nimble as ever.

On the last morning of term, Miss Fox clapped her hands. She said, "Children, you have all been so good. Today we are going for a nice, long walk. I am the leader, so form a line and follow me!"

"We would follow you anywhere, Miss Fox!"
"Bah!" said Lily Lamb. "Bah, silly old Foxy! I am
a free spirit. I will not be led!"

Class Two followed Miss Fox out of the playground and across the road. They followed her over the fields, into the woods and through the trees, all the way to the top of a great tall cliff.

Lily Lamb skipped from side to side at the
end of the line.

"Now, gather round," Miss Fox said. "You are such sweet children. And I'm sure you are all delicious. So who wants to be eaten first?"

"Hee, hee!" everyone giggled. "Isn't Miss Fox Funny?"

But Lily Lamb knew Miss Fox was serious.
So . . .

"I will be first," said Lily Lamb.

Miss Fox said, "Lily, are you being good at last?
Do come quickly, for I am very hungry!"

"But please tell me, will you eat me up snip-snap,
just so?" said Lily Lamb.

"I will gobble you up in a bite!" said Miss Fox.

"Are you sure you can eat all of us?" asked Lily.

"Every single one of you," said Miss Fox. "Wonderful teachers do not have favourites. And now, Lily Lamb, I am going to eat you!"

"Oh no! Miss Fox really means it!" said Class Two. And everyone began to tremble. But not Lily Lamb. She said, "All right, Miss Fox. I'm ready, but you had better open wide."

Miss Fox closed her eyes and opened her mouth as
wide as it would go.
'Now is my chance,' thought Lily.
And with a rush and a push and a shove and a
heave and a puff and a pant . . .

. . . she sent Miss Fox over the cliff.

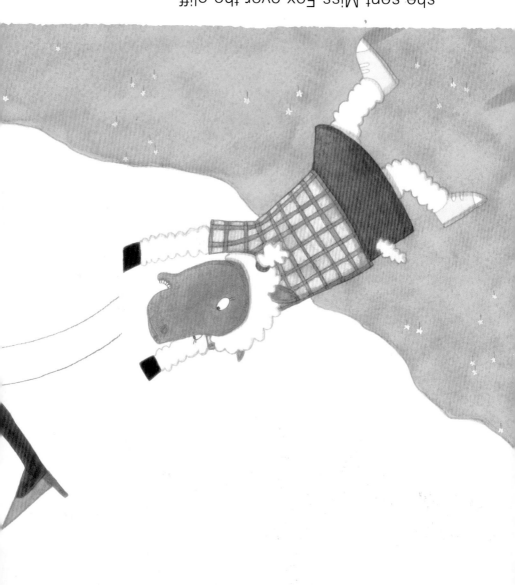

"Goodbye, Foxy!" she shouted. "Isn't being good so boring?"

"You are brave, Lily Lamb!" said Class Two.

"I am, aren't I?" said Lily, smiling her most annoying smile.

It was the first day of school when Miss Fox strolled into Pleasant Town. It looked like a comfy sort of, cosy sort of place.

Miss Fox licked her lips and smiled her best smile.

Collect the TIME TO READ books:

978-1-84780-476-1

978-1-84780-475-4

978-1-84780-477-8

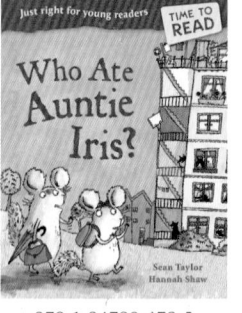
978-1-84780-478-5

978-1-84780-543-0

978-1-84780-544-7

978-1-84780-542-3

978-1-84780-545-4

Frances Lincoln titles are available from all good bookshops.
You can also buy books and find out more about your favourite titles,
authors and illustrators on our website: www.franceslincoln.com